Katie Woo

Katie in the Kitchen

by Fran Manushkin

illustrated by Tammie Lyon

PICTURE WINDOW BOOKS
a capstone imprint

Katie Woo is published by Picture Window Books,
A Capstone Imprint
151 Good Counsel Drive, P.O. Box 669
Mankato, Minnesota, MN 56002
www.capstonepub.com

Printed in the United States of America in Melrose Park, Illinois.
092010
005920R

Library of Congress Cataloging-in-Publication Data
Manushkin, Fran.
    Katie in the kitchen / by Fran Manushkin; illustrated by
Tammie Lyon.
    p. cm. — (Katie Woo)
    ISBN 978-1-4048-5724-7 (library binding)
    [1. Cookery—Fiction. 2. Helpfulness—Fiction. 3. Chinese Americans—Fiction.]
I. Lyon, Tammie, ill. II. Title.
PZ7.M3195Kat 2010
                                                        2009030613
[E]—dc22

Summary: Katie wants to be helpful, and so she starts making dinner on her own.

Art Director: Kay Fraser
Graphic Designer: Emily Harris
Production Specialist: Michelle Biedscheid

Photo Credits
Fran Manushkin, pg. 26
Tammie Lyon, pg. 26

Table of Contents

Chapter 1
Helpful Katie   5

Chapter 2
Cooking Up Trouble   9

Chapter 3
The Ghost   16

Helpful Katie

One day, Katie's mom said, "I'm going next door. Mrs. West has the flu, so I'm going to bring her some soup."

"Can I come and help?"
asked Katie.

"That's not a good idea,"
said her mom. "You might
catch the flu too."

Katie's dad was in the

garage fixing his car.

"Can I help you?" Katie

asked. "I love fixing things."

"No," said her dad.

"These tools are tricky. You

might get hurt."

Katie went back inside, feeling sad.

"I want to help, but nobody will let me," she said to herself. "I know what to do! I'll make dinner. Mom and Dad will be so happy!"

Chapter 2

Cooking Up Trouble

"Mom loves spaghetti," said Katie. "And so do I."

Katie filled a pot with water, three boxes of spaghetti, four cans of tomato sauce, and a jar of olives.

"I think that's enough,"
Katie said. "Turning on the
stove is a no-no, so Mom can
cook this when she comes
back."

"Now I'll make cookies," decided Katie. "Dad loves cookies, and so do I."

Katie poured a bag of flour into a bowl, added two bags of chocolate chips, and stirred it as hard as she could.

Flour flew everywhere.

"It's snowing!" Katie

shouted.

She wrote her name in

flour on the floor. Then she

slipped, and — oops! She fell

down.

"I hurt my knees." Katie sighed. She put on a few Band-Aids.

"These new Band-Aids are fun," she said. So she put a few on her nose too.

"Mom can bake the

cookies when she comes

home," Katie decided.

"Maybe she can clean up

the floor too."

Katie called Pedro and

bragged, "Guess what? I'm

making dinner tonight."

"Cool!" Pedro shouted.

"I'm reading a

great ghost story.

I hope there

aren't any ghosts

in your house."

"No way!" Katie said.

"Goodbye!"

Chapter 3

The Ghost

"I'm not scared of ghosts,"
Katie told herself.

Just then she heard a
weird sound.

"That's not a ghost!" she
decided.

But just in case, she
turned on all the lights. She
also put on her mom's robe
to make herself feel bigger.

Suddenly, a

storm began!

Lightning flashed!

Thunder boomed!

"Storms don't scare me!"

Katie said.

18

She put on her dad's hat to make herself feel braver. The thunder grew louder — and closer.

"Yow!" Katie yelled, and she hid in the closet.

Soon she heard a loud

noise. THUMP! THUMP!

THUMP!

"It's the ghost!" Katie

moaned.

Slowly the closet door

began opening.

"EEEE!" screamed Katie.

"EEEE!" yelled the ghost.

"Mom!" yelled Katie.

"Katie!" shouted her
mom. "You scared me to
death!"

"And this house," said

Katie's mom. "It looks like

an earthquake hit it."

"It was a ghost!" said

Katie quickly.

"Really?" said Katie's

mother. "Are you sure it

wasn't Hurricane Katie?"

"Maybe," Katie confessed.

"But supper is almost ready," Katie bragged. "I've done most of the work."

"Someone's making cookies!" said Katie's dad. "My favorite."

"I'm so glad I could help!" said Katie. "Just ask me — anytime!"

About the Author

Fran Manushkin is the author of many popular picture books, including *How Mama Brought the Spring; Baby, Come Out!; Latkes and Applesauce: A Hanukkah Story;* and *The Tushy Book*. There is a real Katie Woo — she's Fran's great-niece — but she never gets in half the trouble of the Katie Woo in the books. Fran writes on her beloved Mac computer in New York City, without the help of her two naughty cats, Cookie and Goldy.

About the Illustrator

Tammie Lyon began her love for drawing at a young age while sitting at the kitchen table with her dad. She continued her love of art and eventually attended the Columbus College of Art and Design, where she earned a bachelors degree in fine art. After a brief career as a professional ballet dancer, she decided to devote herself full time to illustration. Today she lives with her husband Lee in Cincinnati, Ohio. Her dogs Gus and Dudley keep her company as she works in her studio.

Glossary

confessed (kuhn-FESST)—admitted that you did something wrong

earthquake (URTH-kwayk)—a sudden violent shaking of the ground, caused by a shifting of the Earth's crust

favorite (FAY-vuh-rit)—the thing that is liked best

garage (guh-RAHJ)—a building used to store cars or trucks

hurricane (HUR-uh-kane)—a violent storm with high winds

moaned (MOHND)—made a low, sad sound

spaghetti (spuh-GET-ee)—long, thin strands of pasta made of flour and water and cooked by boiling

Discussion Questions

1. Do you like to cook? What sort of foods do you make?

2. Have you ever thought there was a ghost in your house? What happened?

3. Do you think Katie was being helpful? Why or why not?

Writing Prompts

1. Katie tried to make spaghetti, one of her favorite meals. Write the recipe for one of your favorite meals.

2. Katie feels scared when thinking about ghosts and hearing the storm. What are you scared of? List five things.

3. When the storm scared Katie, she put on her dad's hat to feel braver. What makes you feel brave when you are scared? Write a sentence or two to explain why it makes you feel brave.

Having Fun with Katie Woo

In *Katie in the Kitchen*, Katie starts dinner all by herself. Cooking is fun! Spaghetti is a hard recipe to make all on your own. But you can make this easy snack with hardly any help. Just be sure to ask a grown-up for permission, and always wash your hands before cooking.

Yogurt Parfait for One

Ingredients:

- 1 cup vanilla yogurt
- 1 cup assorted washed berries (strawberries, blueberries, and raspberries)
- 1/2 cup granola

Other things you need:

- a glass
- spoons

What you do:

1. Scoop half of the yogurt into your glass.

2. Add half of the berries.

3. Top with half of the granola.

4. Repeat the layers, ending with the granola. Serve with a spoon.

Yogurt parfaits can be made with a lot of different add-ins. Try using other fruits and cereals. For a special, once-in-a-while treat, you could add crushed cookies or mini chocolate chips. **Yum!**